The Demon Cat
and other strange tales

by
Aaron Percifull

Watermill Press

Contents of this edition copyright © 1983 by Watermill Press, Mahwah, New Jersey

Printed in the United States of America

Illustrations by James R. Odbert

ISBN 0-89375-827-2

Contents

A Walk on the Red Cliff

A full moon crept over the Red Cliff. Near the edge, shadows danced in the pale light. A sudden shriek split the night air. It was followed by a dull thud on the rocks below.

"We found your brother," Sheriff Jones told Sam Blake the next day. "He was on the rocks below the Red Cliff."

"Jerry's dead?" Sam said. His eyes filled with tears and anger. "Who did it?"

Sheriff Jones touched Sam on the shoulder, shaking his head. "We found this note in his vest."

Sam grabbed the note, hoping that it wasn't his brother's writing. But the note had been typed. It read:

> *I stole bank funds and lost the money. I can't face the thought of prison. I'm sorry.*
>
> *Jerry*

At Jerry's funeral, Todd Crane came over to Sam. Todd was a cousin who had taken control of the Blake Bank after Jerry's death. It had been Todd who discovered that Jerry had taken the money.

"I'm sorry," Todd said. "I always felt that Jerry was such an honest man. It's too bad it had to end this way."

"Why would he do it?" Sam asked.

"I think it was an oil deal," Todd said. "I guess the well just never came in."

"That sounds more like your style," Sam said. He had never trusted Todd and neither had Jerry.

Todd's eyes narrowed, but he managed a tight smile. "I don't fool around with other folks' money," he said.

Manning Rubin walked over towards them and nodded at Sam. Manning was the new vice president at the bank. At one time, he'd been Todd's partner.

Sam watched the men stroll away from the graveyard. Something told him that these men knew more than they said they knew about Jerry's crime.

That night, Sam went up to the Red Cliff to look around. He searched the area. But he didn't find a thing. After a while, he made his way off the cliff.

Sam was almost down when he glanced back at the Red Cliff. It was a strange, cloudy night that hid the moon. But then, a sharp wind shoved the clouds free. In the pale light, Sam thought he saw something walking near the edge of the cliff. It seemed to stare at Sam for a moment. Then, it was gone.

"My mind is playing tricks," Sam said. But he wasn't too sure.

A few days later, Sam was sitting in front of the barber shop. Dave Jenkins came into town, and he seemed upset.

"I saw something up on the Red Cliff last night," he told Sam. "I think it was – a ghost."

Soon, the word spread in town that the Red Cliff was haunted. Folks began to believe that it was Jerry's ghost up on the cliff.

"Do you believe all that talk about Jerry's ghost?" Sam asked Todd one day near the bank.

"Not a bit," Todd said. "Excuse me. I've got work to do."

Sam stared at his cousin. Again, he felt Todd was hiding something. All of a sudden, Sam walked around the side of the bank. It was as if something were pulling him. Sam stopped under Todd's office. The window was open, and Sam heard two voices inside.

"When do we get the cash?" Manning Rubin said.

"We'll dig it up as soon as all of this ghost business dies down. That's the plan."

"The plan was just to scare Jerry on the cliff. Remember?"

"Shut up!" Todd hissed. "Don't ever say that again. We did what we had to do."

9

Sam stopped under Todd's office.

Sam's ears burned. He wanted to smash Todd into a thousand pieces. But when his rage passed, he knew what had happened.

Todd and Manning had needed cash. They took the money from the bank, but Jerry caught them. They took Jerry up to the Red Cliff to scare him into calling the theft a bank loan. Jerry wouldn't do it, and he was tossed off the cliff. Later, they put the note in Jerry's vest to explain it all.

But how can I prove it? thought Sam.

Sam went back to his house and found some of Jerry's old letters. Carefully, he copied his brother's writing to make a note. It read:

Meet me on the Red Cliff tonight.
It's not over.

Jerry.

11

Maybe this will scare them into going up there, Sam thought. He found Dave Jenkins in town and told him part of his plan.

"I want you to slip this note under Todd's door just after dark," Sam said. "Then meet me at the Red Cliff."

Sam found Sheriff Jones in his office. "You've got to come with me," Sam pleaded. "I know it all sounds crazy. But you've got to trust me."

It was well past dark when Sam and Sheriff Jones reached the top of the Red Cliff. They hid in the bushes near the edge of the cliff.

About an hour passed before two voices came up the trail. Sam nudged Sheriff Jones when Todd and Manning came into the clearing. Todd held a note in his trembling hands.

"I tell you, it's Jerry's writing," Todd

said. "I'm sure of it."

"How could that be?"

"I don't know. I just don't know."

A form moved out of the bushes. It wore a huge, black cloak and walked towards the two men.

"Todd, look!" Manning screamed.

Two bloody hands came out of the cloak. "Give the money back," the figure moaned.

Todd and Manning shrank back in fear. "Do what it says," Manning cried. He ran to the base of the largest tree on the cliff. He dug with his bare hands near the trunk of the tree.

"Stop it, you fool," Todd shouted as he pulled out his gun. He turned and faced the form in the cloak. "I got rid of you before. I'll do it again."

Todd was about to pull the trigger when the barrel of a shotgun nudged his

"Give me the money back," the figure moaned.

back. "Drop it," Sheriff Jones said.

Sheriff Jones handcuffed Todd while Sam climbed out of the cloak.

"So it was *you!*" Todd yelled. "I thought as much."

Sam walked over to Manning, who had stayed by the tree. He led Manning back to the sheriff. Then he went back to the tree. He felt under the earth and found a large tin box. Inside was the missing money from the bank.

"Good work, Sam," Sheriff Jones said. "A lot of folks will be happy to get this back."

The sheriff led Todd and Manning down the trail. A few moments later, Sam heard someone running towards him. Dave Jenkins was out of breath as he reached Sam.

"Am I too late?" Dave panted. "I've still got that note you wanted me to give

Todd. Is he here?"

Sam stared at Dave's hand. In it was the note Sam had written. Then Sam glanced at the note that Todd had dropped on the ground.

"If you didn't give him my note, where did they get this one?" Sam said. He grabbed the note off the ground, and his hands began to shake. The note read:

I walk the Red Cliff until the
truth is told.

Jerry.

It was Jerry's handwriting that bothered Sam the most. Then the wind whistled through the trees. It seemed to whisper, "Thanks for the help."

To Beat the Devil

An old man sat in front of the fireplace of a large, nicely furnished room. For quite some time, Jack Blaine gazed into the flames. Then he slowly looked up at a picture above the fireplace. It was a portrait of himself as a young man.

Jack studied the picture. He had

never been a handsome man. But he had been very sharp and smart. He had been the kind of man who always knew what he wanted. And he knew how to get it — one way or another.

Jack stared into the painted eyes. He smiled. But the eyes didn't smile back. Instead, they glared coldly at all who thought they could get the better of Jack Blaine.

Jack thought about his younger days. "I was the best," Jack said aloud. "Nobody put anything over on me. Con games, cards, oil deals, land schemes, scams — it didn't matter."

He raised his hand and pointed at his portrait. "*I was the best!*" he croaked again. Then his strength gave out. His hand flopped into his lap. Jack stared at his hands. They were brown-spotted and blue-veined with age.

"I just got old," he muttered to himself. He looked at his picture again and let out a soft moan.

"I would give anything to be like that again," he said bitterly.

"That can be arranged, Mr. Blaine," a voice answered.

Jack looked around. Standing by his chair was a handsome young man in a business suit. The man had piercing, coal-black eyes.

"Who let you in here?" Jack demanded.

The stranger smiled and walked to the fireplace. He glanced at the painting. Then he turned to face Jack. "Mr. Blaine," he said, "my name is Mr. Natas. I have come to offer you a little business deal."

Mr. Natas removed the portrait from the wall and held it near Jack. "Do you really want to be like him? I'm sure we

The man had piercing coal-black eyes.

can work something out."

"What are you talking about?" Jack said loudly. "You can't make me young again. That's crazy!"

"Why don't you look at your hand?"

Jack raised his hand and gasped. The wrinkles and spots were gone. His hand felt strong again. "How did — ?" he began in amazement.

Natas flashed a smile, cutting him off. "Now don't worry about that. Let's concentrate on the details of my offer. Quite simply," Natas said, clasping his hands together, "how would you like to be the best again, Mr. Blaine? I'm offering you the chance to go back and live it all another time."

"You can *do* that?" Jack asked greedily. "How? When?"

"As soon as you sign this," Natas said. He snapped his fingers, and at once a paper appeared in his hands. Natas proudly handed it to Jack. "Sign it – in blood."

Jack pulled out his reading glasses to study the agreement. He looked up after a moment. His eyes were shining when he spoke.

"You mean you won't take my soul until I have the chance to do it all?"

"That's right."

Jack laughed and clapped his hands. "I'll sign it right now."

"I know you're doing the right thing," Natas said. His smile gleamed in the firelight. He handed Jack a thin metal rod with a sharp point.

Jack paused for a second to look at Natas. But then he shrugged, pricked his finger, and pressed it to the contract.

There was a huge flash of light and smoke. Suddenly, Jack found himself on a street corner in a small town.

What's going on? he wondered. *Everything looks fifty years old.*

Jack turned and saw his reflection in a store window. A young man with hard eyes stared back at him.

Is that really me? Jack thought. *Yes, and now I remember.* He felt in his pockets for a worthless deed. *I'm on my way to sell some land to Old Man Cringle.*

Jack gazed at the deed and laughed. *That old fool,* Jack thought. *I just wish I could see the look on his face when he finds out his farm is under a swamp.*

Jack rushed down the street to Cringle's office. He went into the office. But he had a surprise waiting.

"There you are, Mr. Blaine," Cringle said at the door. "I was afraid you wouldn't drop by. It seems that there is a slight problem with the land that you tried to sell me."

"What?" Jack asked.

"I sent two of my men out to check on that property. They tell me that the land is under water. You're nothing but a crook!"

"You've got it all wrong," Jack insisted. But at that moment, the office door opened and Sheriff Stone came into the room.

"You had better come with me, Blaine," Sheriff Stone said roughly. "I've got a room waiting for you."

Jack stared at Cringle with wide eyes. "I don't understand," he said. "You have to buy the land. That's the way it was before."

Cringle gave Jack a strange look and shook his head.

"Let's go," Sheriff Stone said. He grabbed Jack's arm. Jack struggled to

"You had better come with me, Blaine,"
Sheriff Stone said.

get loose, but the sheriff kept a firm, tight grip on him.

"But it's not supposed to be like this," Jack howled as Sheriff Stone led him away. He was taken to the county jail, and shortly afterward, he was found guilty of fraud.

Jack sat staring at the bars of the cell that would be his home for the next twenty years.

What went wrong? he asked himself. *I should have made a fortune from that land deal.* "Natas!" he screamed. "You tricked me!"

Suddenly, Natas appeared in Jack's cell. "No I did not, Mr. Blaine," Natas smiled. "I merely offered you the *chance* to do it all again. But, my friend," Natas said, laughing, "nothing was ever guaranteed."

Demon Cat

"Isn't he adorable?" Cindy said. She cuddled the black kitten. Its green eyes shone brightly. It did not purr. "Look, Dad, isn't he cute?"

Dad frowned. "Yes, Cindy, he's cute, but he can't stay. You know the rule."

"Daddy, please," Cindy pleaded, "it'll be different this time. I'm older now,

27

and I'll take care of him. I promise I will."

"Well, sweetheart," Dad said, "that kitten seems to like it here. But, remember, you have to take care of him. If you don't, the kitten must leave."

Cindy was very happy. "Oh, Daddy, thank you! Don't worry, I'll take good care of him." She petted the kitten. It looked at her with its green eyes. It didn't purr.

Mom poured Dad a cup of coffee. "I was talking to Helen Moran today," she began. "She lives across the street."

Dad nodded and picked up the newspaper.

Mom went on, "She has heard that this house is haunted. What do you think about that, Walter?"

Dad looked up from his paper. "You know I don't believe in ghosts, Lois," he began. "This house is not haunted. No house is haunted. Have you seen a single ghost? Have you heard one? No, of course not. That's because there aren't any. There never will be any."

Dad stood up and drank the last of his coffee. "I've got to go. I'll be late for work." He kissed Cindy and Mom goodbye.

Cindy heard the car start. She stroked the kitten. "What shall I call him?"

"Your kitten?" Mom asked. "Oh, I don't know."

"I think I'll call him Stormy," Cindy said.

Weeks passed and Stormy grew. At first, the cat seemed normal. But soon, Cindy noticed some strange things about her pet. For one thing, the cat never purred. And his eyes were so green, they seemed to glow. Also, he never really played; he destroyed. Cindy

29

bought him toys. Cloth toys got shredded in hours. Plastic toys sometimes lasted a few days.

Stormy grew worse every day. He liked to swing from the living-room drapes. Soon the drapes were in shreds. He clawed the sofa to ribbons. He loved to knock over waste-paper cans and drag the mess all over the room.

Things got much worse. Stormy took over Cindy's room. It was a shambles. She couldn't leave anything out. It would get shredded or torn or chewed to pieces. Before long, Cindy couldn't enter her room. The cat would sit on the bed. (The mattress was chewed and torn. The stuffing was coming out.) If Cindy came near Stormy, he would hiss and spit.

Dad had tried to get rid of Stormy. The first time, Dad got badly clawed and bitten. The next time, he called the

*Stormy loved to drag the mess
all over the room.*

police. They came with people from the animal shelter. A man with heavy leather gloves caught Stormy. The cat screeched and struggled. The man put him in a canvas bag. At last, Stormy was gone.

The next day, Stormy was back. How or why was a mystery. Dad opened the door to go to work, and there was the cat. He zoomed past Dad to Cindy's room, and there he stayed.

That night, Dad looked tired. He ate dinner slowly. "I don't know what to do," he said. "I don't know anymore. That cat is ruining us. We may have to move."

Cindy was afraid to speak. But she knew she must. "Dad, I've got an idea. It's not my idea, really. It's Freddie's."

"Freddie?" Dad asked. "Oh, yes—your boyfriend."

"Yes, Dad. He says that Stormy really

belongs to a witch. That's why Stormy is so mean. The witch lived here. Now she wants her cat back."

Dad looked at Mom. He shook his head. "What's she talking about, Lois?"

"Freddie claims his grandmother can speak with the dead. She goes into a trance and talks to them. She holds regular séances. This witch keeps coming to her and demanding her cat. Freddie figures it's Stormy. Who knows, Walter? He might be right."

"Really, Lois!" Dad said. "This is ridiculous!"

"Yes, Walter," Mom said. "It's ridiculous, but it may be true. You remember those rumors. People believe this house is haunted. Well, maybe it is."

"So what if it is true?" Dad said.

"Freddie's grandmother will hold a séance," Cindy said.

"Yes," Mom added. "She'll hold a séance right here. She'll call the witch. If the story is true, then the witch will come and take Stormy."

Dad nodded. "O.K. I think it's stupid, and it won't work. But let's have the séance." Mom and Cindy smiled at each other.

The séance was held when the moon was full. Freddie's grandmother, Mrs. Foster, arrived early. She had to prepare the room.

Soon the room was ready. Candles were lit. The lights were out. Mrs. Foster called the others in. Everyone sat in a circle around the dining-room table. Mrs. Foster sat at the head. She slowly closed her eyes.

"Join hands," she ordered. "Put your hands on top of the table. We now form a living circle. Whatever happens, do *not* break the circle! Keep the circle together at all costs. It is our only hope."

Mrs. Foster's head jerked. Her whole body shivered. Then a voice came from her. It was not her voice. It was harsh and demanding. "Where is he? Where is my pet? Where is my companion? Release him! Return him! He's mine, mine, mine!"

A wind came from nowhere. The candles flickered. Suddenly, Stormy jumped onto the center of the table. He arched his back and hissed.

Mrs. Foster's body shook. Again, the strange voice spoke. "Aha! There you are, my pretty! I've been searching for you. Come away! Come away! Come away!"

The candles flared and went out. Mrs. Foster screamed. Dad started to get up, but Mom and Cindy held him. The circle

"Where is he? Where is my pet?"

could not be broken. Minutes went by. Then Mrs. Foster spoke. She sounded breathless. "It is finished. She has gone. She has taken her companion. Your troubles are over.... You may now break the circle."

Dad turned on the lights. He started looking for Stormy. He looked everywhere, but Stormy was gone. Dad came to Mrs. Foster, who was sipping a cup of tea.

"I don't know what you did," he said. "I don't know how you did it. But that cat is gone. Thank you!"

Mrs. Foster put down her cup. "That's funny," she said. "I can't remember a thing. I never do. Why did you have me here tonight?"

Mom and Dad smiled at each other. They both hugged Cindy.

Lake Fear

Annie, Phil, and Mike looked out over the lake. "You were right, Mike," Annie said. "It's very quiet here."

"It sure is," Mike replied. "People say nothing lives in Lake Fear – nothing except the monster."

Annie felt a shiver run up her spine. "The monster – that's creepy!"

"And we're going to find him," Mike said. He clamped the motor to the end of the boat.

"Wait—our lunch!" Annie said, running back to the car. She came back with a picnic basket. "We can't forget food for the monster," she said with a smile.

The three put on life jackets. Mike started the motor. They glided out over the lake. The water was very still and dark. The only sound was the putt-putt of the motor.

Mike said, "Keep your eyes open. Annie, watch off the front. Phil, take the right and left. I'll check the rear every once in a while." Mike steered them out toward the center of the lake.

"What are we looking for?" Annie asked.

"A monster, silly," Phil said to her.

"I *know* that," Annie replied. "But

"We can't forget food for the monster,"
Annie said with a smile.

what kind of monster? I mean, is it big and green, or is it long and purple? Is it yellow with flaming eyes, or is it. . ."

Phil interrupted her. "Listen, nobody knows for sure what it looks like. But everybody knows it's here—everybody!"

"I still think you made it up," she said.

"Phil is right," Mike said. "It's here somewhere, waiting. My grandfather saw it, but that was fifty years ago."

"Yeah," said Annie, "sure. So it's probably dead by now anyhow—*if* it ever existed."

"Quiet!" Mike ordered. "Listen. . . . Do you hear anything?"

The three listened. They were about halfway across the lake. An island loomed in front of them. It was dark and covered with fog.

"Some people say it lives there," Mike said. He pointed to the island. "There, and in the water nearby.... Listen!"

"Over the sound of the motor?" Annie asked. "What can we hear?"

"*Shhh!*" said Mike. "Just listen!" Mike, Phil, and Annie listened as the water slapped at the sides of the boat.

The boat slid over the water. Shapes appeared without warning.

"Look!" Annie said breathlessly. "Take a look over there!" She pointed to a curved form. It seemed to move—or did it? It was barely above the water.

Mike moved the boat closer to the mysterious form. "Poke it with an oar, Phil," he said.

Phil thrust the oar forward. It cut the fog like a sword. The oar made contact, and the thing swayed gently. As Phil pushed harder, something seemed to groan and scrape. Then more of the thing began to appear.

"Oh, no!" Annie gasped. She started to scream.

When she stopped, all was silent. The thing in the water floated peacefully.

"It's just a submerged tree," said Mike. "It must have broken off when Phil shoved it."

"Darn it, Mike!" Annie shouted. "You knew that all along, didn't you?"

Mike was silent until the small boat neared the far shore of the lake. "Let's beach the boat there. We can eat on that point."

Mike put the oars in the locks and rowed to the shore. The three friends got out and made for the point. They ate in silence. Annie sat against a tree. The tree hung over the water. The boys sat facing her.

"Well," said Annie finally, "Don't you think this joke has gone far enough?

Monster? Ha! The only monster here is.... Phil? What's the matter?"

Phil was turning pale. He pointed at Annie. "Oh, no!" he exclaimed.

Mike got slowly to his feet. He said, "Annie, I want you to come to me. Move slowly. Make no sudden movements." There was horror in his eyes.

Annie just laughed. She took another bite of chicken salad. "Come on, guys. Cut it out. Enough is enough. It isn't funny anymore and..."

Annie screamed as a green, slimy hand touched her arm. Terrified, she ran toward the boat. The others ran after her. The monster's head appeared by the tree. It was half human, half lizard. Green slime dripped from its brow. Red, intelligent eyes watched the three running away. The creature slipped back into the water.

Mike, Phil, and Annie reached the boat. "Get in," Mike said. "Hurry!" He started the motor.

They headed out into the lake. The boat began to rock, and a green hand appeared over the side. The monster had hold of the boat.

"Get him, Phil," Mike said. "Hit him with the oar." Phil grabbed the oar. He bashed the monster's hand. It held on still. Phil hit it again. The hand slipped away. The boat rocked violently.

The motor sputtered. After a few putts, it stopped. The monster's head emerged near them. It howled at them in anger. Annie said, "If it breathes fire, we're finished."

Mike cursed the motor. He tried to start it. Once, twice—nothing. The monster went underwater. It emerged a foot from the boat.

The monster's head emerged near them.

Again Mike tried the motor. It coughed and stopped. The monster came closer. Mike gave the motor cord a savage tug. The motor sprang to life. He swung the boat away from the monster. It howled after them, then sank under the surface.

Mike headed straight for the shore. The monster appeared several times. Again and again, they dodged it and fought it off.

Slowly, it fell a little behind them. When they reached the shore, Mike said, "Run! Leave the boat! Leave everything! Just run for the car!" The three leaped into the shallow water. They splashed ashore, then ran for the car.

Annie looked back. The monster was at the boat. He lifted it high in the air. *Smash!* It came down on the rocks. Over and over, the monster threw the boat to the ground.

Mike reached the car first. He started the motor. The others hopped in. The tires squealed as they sped away. They heard a crash behind them. The monster was still throwing the boat around.

"No one will believe this," Phil said.

"Who cares?" said Annie. "We're alive, Phil. We're *alive!*"

The Legend of Joe Fargo and Lem

"How would you like to bite down on a hook?" Lem asked.

"Not very much," Joe Fargo had to admit. "Not very much at all."

"Well, a fish doesn't either," Lem said.

Lem was asking for Joe to give up

fishing. Joe promised Lem he would think about it. It was something that would take very careful thought.

Give up fishing? Joe had fished all his life. His father had taken him fishing the day he was born. And he had caught his first fish when he was three.

It just didn't seem possible that Joe could give up fishing. But he couldn't ignore Lem's point of view. Lem was Joe's best friend. They had been friends for three years. That was when Lem had saved Joe's life. Now Joe thought back to that day.

It was a Thursday. On Thursdays, the men always met in Pete Gifford's barn for a friendly game or two of cards. Joe was there as usual. And, as usual, he was winning. He was ahead by 150 points. Naturally this made the rest of the men edgy.

Then Seth Knowles made a discovery. It was a small discovery, but it was enough to get the men upset, edgy as they were. What Seth noticed was a small bit of cardboard sticking out of Joe's sleeve. You can imagine how surprised they all were to find it was an ace of hearts.

So they turned Joe upside down and shook him a bit. This produced six more aces and a king.

"Now that," said Seth, "accounts for most of Joe's good luck."

Without another word, the men carried Joe to the river, threw him in, and left. They never bothered to ask Joe if he could swim or not.

Joe couldn't swim, which left him with quite a problem. He shouted and he thrashed about. And then Lem came along and saved him.

Joe shouted and he thrashed about.

Lem swam up under Joe. "Hold onto my fin," he said. And Joe did what he was told. Then Lem swam to the shore where Joe could grab the root of a tree. Joe pulled himself up and fell on the bank gasping.

"You should learn to swim," Lem said, "especially if you're going to cheat at cards."

Joe agreed. He said he would do that the first chance he got. And he thanked Lem for his help and kindness. It was only then that he realized he was talking to a fish.

"Call me Lem," Lem said.

At first, Joe thought he had drowned. *I am dead*, he said to himself. *And I have come back to life as a fish.* He felt himself all over. No, he wasn't a fish. He was also pretty sure that he wasn't dead.

Joe peered into the river. He found

himself eye to eye with the biggest catfish he had ever seen. From whiskers to tail, the fish was at least five feet long. And he had to be 150 pounds if he was an ounce.

"Lem?" Joe said.

"That's my name," the fish answered.

"You'll have to forgive me," Joe said. "But I've never met a talking catfish before."

"It figures," Lem said. "But you'll get used to it after a while."

Joe did get used to it, and he and Lem became good friends. They would talk about many things. Sooner or later, they had to come to talk about fishing. As I said, it was a big part of Joe's life.

"Just suppose," Lem said, "that instead of saving you that day, I had eaten you. There are fish who do that sort of thing, you know."

Joe shuddered at the thought. Then he thought of himself gobbling on a plate of fried fish. Being a friend of Lem's, he suddenly felt terribly cruel.

"But wait a minute, Lem," Joe said. "Fish eat fish, too."

Lem had to admit that was true. Fish *do* eat other fish. When he was small, he was almost eaten himself, by a large bass. "It's a dog-eat-dog world," Lem sighed.

"Fish-eat-fish," Joe corrected him. And then Lem began to cry.

"There's just so much cruelty in the world," he sobbed. "I just thought that maybe you . . ." he stopped to blow his nose. "I thought that maybe you and I could be different. I'm a vegetarian, you know."

To prove the point, Lem swallowed a large water lily, pad and all.

"I'm not much for water lilies myself,"

Joe said. But he did hate to see Lem upset. "I'll sleep on it," he promised. And that's exactly what he did. He lay back on the grass to think. The sun was warm and he soon fell asleep.

Joe was awakened sometime later by men shouting. Mixed with the shouting was a loud thrashing and splashing.

"Whooo-eee!" one of the men shouted. "Look at the size of that fish! Hang on now, men!" It was Seth Knowles and three others.

Fearing the worst, Joe ran down to the riverbank. What he saw made his blood run cold. The four men were struggling with a net. In the net was Lem, fighting for his life.

"Stop that! Let go of that fish!" Joe shouted.

The men weren't about to let go of their catch. And they said so.

"Look at the size of that fish!"

57

Joe whipped out his knife and dove into the river. With two quick slashes, he cut the net. Lem was free. But now Joe found himself drowning once again. He still hadn't learned to swim. He thrashed about and shouted for help.

"Serves you right," the men jeered at him. "You had to ruin our catch. Go ahead and drown."

In his panic, Lem had tried to swim away. He was some distance down river when he heard Joe shouting. Not one to desert a friend in need, he turned back. He dove deep into the channel. When he reached Joe, he surfaced and shouted, "Grab hold, Joe. Quick!"

Joe grabbed a fin and held his breath. Lem made a quick dive. Man and fish disappeared together under the surface of the water.

The four fishermen never could agree

what had happened. One said Joe had gone crazy and drowned. Another said he had been killed and eaten by the giant catfish. Still another thought he had seen Joe riding on the catfish's back. But he was afraid to say so.

Word got around that Joe Fargo was probably dead. When he didn't show up for the card game at Gifford's barn two weeks in a row, his friends were sure of it. They held a nice service in his memory. Joe was fine and honest and would be missed, they all said.

The truth is, Joe and Lem just went off together. They found a nice pond deep in the woods where no one would bother them. And they lived quietly.

Joe gave up fishing which made Lem very happy. Now they were both vege-tarians. The pond was filled with flowers and grass. And Joe became used

to acorns and wild fruits and vege-
tables.

It was a good life. There was no end to
the things they found to talk about. And
on Thursdays, they would play cards.

Terror in the Woods

"I'm sorry I can't go with you guys," Bill said, "but this is an emergency. The milking machine broke, and my family has to help my dad milk the whole herd by hand!" Bill winced at the thought.

Ted laughed at him. Bill looked so sad. Ted, Sam, and Bill had been looking forward to the weekend. Now that Sam could drive, it was easy to get away. Ted's parents had a cabin in the woods. They were going to spend the weekend there.

Sam said, "What's a little milking? You're a farm boy."

Bill took a friendly swipe at Sam. "Aw, cut it out. I haven't milked in years. I'll probably get blisters."

"Think of the poor cows!" Ted said. They all laughed. "We're sorry you can't come with us. Next time, buddy. O.K.?"

"Sure," Bill replied. "Next time." He walked them to the car. "You guys be careful."

"Oh, yeah!" Sam said. "We've got to watch out for all those big bad bears in the woods."

Bill smiled at them. "I won't be there to protect you from Bigfoot."

Sam started the car. Ted said, "Some

protection you'd be! Well, take care. We'll say hello to Bigfoot for you."

Sam and Ted drove for about an hour. Sam turned onto an unmarked dirt road. It wound up the hill, then stopped. There was barely room to turn the car around. Sam parked and got out. "It's time for a hike," Ted said.

The cabin was about a mile down a dirt path. The boys put on their backpacks. They started hiking.

"Too bad Bill isn't here," Sam said.

"Yeah," Ted added. "It's the first time he's not with us."

Staring at the ground, Sam was suddenly silent, "Ted!" he whispered. "Look!"

Ted's eyes followed Sam's gaze. He saw a footprint. It was much too huge to belong to a human being. "Do you think it's a bear's print?" Ted asked.

"Do you think it's a bear's print?" Ted asked.

"It can't be," Sam replied. "You know we don't have bears that size—not around here."

"Maybe it's lost. Maybe it got here by mistake."

"Maybe it's Bigfoot."

Ted felt a shiver creep up his spine. "Let's get to the cabin—now."

The two walked on in uneasy silence. Finally Sam said, "If it is Bigfoot . . ."

"Don't be ridiculous," Ted interrupted.

The path opened onto a small clearing. The cabin took up most of the space. It looked very safe, like a log fortress.

"Welcome," said Ted as he opened the door. "Welcome to the Wild West." He and Sam threw their gear down. "We'll sleep in front of the fire tonight, O.K.?"

Well, Sam thought, *it suits me. I don't want to be alone tonight. Not with Bigfoot or whatever it is out there. I guess*

Ted feels the same. Sam said, "Yeah, Ted, it's going to be a cold one. The fire will feel good."

After dinner, Sam lit a roaring fire. The two boys crawled into their sleeping bags.

Sam stared at the ceiling. The firelight made strange shadows there, like bats flying around. Far away, a wolf howled. Slowly, Sam dozed off.

BOOM! . . . BOOM! BOOM!

Sam woke with a start. He felt cold with sweat.

BOOM! BOOM!

Something shook the cabin door.

"Ted!" Sam whispered frantically.

"I'm awake," Ted whispered. "I thought that noise was you."

"No," Sam said. "I'm right here." The pounding repeated itself.

"Throw some wood on the fire." Ted

ordered. "I'll light a lantern. And get a heavy stick or something."

Sam quickly fed the fire until it roared. He picked up a log, then he looked up at Ted. Ted's left hand held a lantern. His right hand held a frying pan.

BOOM! BOOM! BOOM! The door shook violently.

"Come on!" Ted said. The two boys moved to a window and Ted held up the lantern. "The light might scare it away."

"What is it?" Sam said, hoping that Ted knew.

"I . . . I don't know," Ted answered.

A figure appeared in front of them. It was close and coming closer. The light seemed to attract it. It was big, like a bear, but its fur was long and matted. Long, stringy hair covered its face and body. The creature growled and threatened.

The creature growled and threatened.

"Bigfoot!" Sam exclaimed. "What are we going to do?"

Ted moved away from the window. "I don't know. I guess we wait for it to leave."

BOOM! BOOM!

The boys stared at the door. It wasn't locked. There was no lock. The doorknob began to turn.

"Get ready," Ted said. He gripped the frying pan tightly. "Stand there, behind the door. I'll take the other side. If I miss...he's all yours."

The door slowly opened. It seemed to take forever. Ted raised the frying pan. The big, hairy thing stood there. Ted thought, *I must do it! I must!* Then...

"Stop, Ted! Don't, please!" the monster said. "Stop! It's me, Bill!"

Ted lowered the frying pan. He said, "You almost got clobbered, buddy." His voice was shaking. "Come on out, Sam, it's all right. It's just Bill, dressed up in a gorilla suit."

Sam came out from behind the door. Bill was pulling off his monster hood. "I really fooled you two!" he said. He grinned broadly.

"You planned this all along?" Ted asked.

"Yeah," Bill said. "I even got my brother to drive me." He really enjoyed the idea. "Boy, were you two scared!"

"Have you got your gear with you?" Ted asked. Bill nodded. "Well, go get it," Ted said. "That is, if you want to stay."

Bill returned with his backpack. He took off the costume. "Help me with this, will you? There's a zipper in back." Sam worked the zipper down. "I've been planning for weeks," Bill said. "I got this old gorilla suit."

Sam said, "Where are the feet?"

"I really fooled you two!" Bill said.

"What?" Bill said.

"The feet for the gorilla suit."

"I left them home. Too clumsy."

"Oh," said Sam, "I get it. You made those tracks earlier."

"What tracks?" Bill asked.

Ted and Sam looked at each other. Ted said, "The tracks by the path, Bill. The tracks you made to scare us. The Bigfoot tracks."

Bill stepped out of the costume. "I told you, I left the feet at home. I have sneakers on, see?" He held up his feet for inspection. He looked from Ted to Sam. Neither said a word.

The Man Who Didn't Believe

It was a howling November night. The boys gathered around the old stove in Mason's General Store.

"Well," Sam Butler said, "Tom Jenkins swears he saw the green light again up on Hollow Ridge."

"I believe it," said Lem Johnson. "Folks say it's the ghost of Mason's aunt, Lou Ann Turner, who froze to death."

Joe Gibbs had been leaning back in his chair. But Lem's words made him laugh and almost fall over.

"Ghost," Joe Gibbs scoffed. "There's no such thing. Old Tom's eyes aren't what they used to be."

"There's nothing wrong with Tom's eyes," Lem said. "Besides, he's not the only one who has seen the green light. A lot of folks have. Right, Sam?"

"You bet," Sam agreed.

"Well, that's the difference between you and me," Joe said scornfully. "I've got education. Anybody with education knows that ghosts aren't real."

"Excuse me," Lem answered, "but I know what I'm talking about."

Joe gave Lem a challenging stare.

"Well, maybe you'd like to put your money where your mouth is. The Owens place is supposed to be haunted, isn't it?"

"Maybe," Lem said with a twinkle in his eyes.

"All right," Joe said firmly. He reached into his pocket and brought out a greasy twenty-dollar bill. "This says I'll spend tomorrow night there."

Sam and Lem looked at each other and laughed.

The next evening at sunset, Joe walked slowly up to the deserted Owens mansion. He lit a candle and went into the old, dark house. By the dim light, he was able to find a spot that was out of the draft. He tossed down his bedroll and tried to get comfortable. It would be a long night.

Joe kept busy by writing notes in his diary. It was midnight when he looked at his watch. He hadn't seen or heard a thing that was the least bit like a ghost.

"Lem's just crazy," he told himself with a laugh. "I just can't wait to see—"

Just then, a loud crash came from the next room. It was followed by the sound of chains being dragged across the floor.

Joe's face turned pale. He imagined that something horrible was coming for him in the dark. He started to shake when the chains suddenly stopped rattling. Then Joe heard a strange voice coming from the next room.

"This house is perfect, Kincaid. The cops will never look for us here. Come on, we've got to get out of these chains."

Joe peered through a crack in the wall. A silvery shaft of moonlight lit up the next room. Joe could clearly see two men in prison clothes. They were trying to cut the heavy chains that trailed from their ankles.

I've got to get out of here, Joe thought. Softly, he climbed through a window and ran across a clearing into the woods. It was quite dark beneath the branches, but Joe soon saw a strange light. A young girl with a lantern came gliding out of the dark.

"Come with me," she said. "I will help you find your way."

"That's very nice of you, miss," Joe said, happy to have found a light to help him get out of the woods. He followed the girl along a narrow path that led out to the main road.

It's very strange that this young lady just appeared out of nowhere, Joe thought to himself as he trudged along.

"Excuse me, miss," Joe called out in

"Come with me," the young girl said.
"I will help you find your way."

his friendliest voice. "Where did you come from? Do you live over in the valley?"

The girl suddenly stopped and pointed. Joe looked and found that they had reached the main road. He turned to thank the young girl. But when he glanced around, she was gone. He searched for the lantern's light. But it was quite dark again.

That's strange, Joe thought as he rushed back to town. Joe found the sheriff and told him about the two men who were up at the Owens place. Then he went home.

The next night, Joe strolled to Mason's General Store. He found all of his friends, as usual, sitting around the old stove.

"Well, here's your twenty, Lem," Joe said. He pulled out a crisp new bill from his bulging wallet. "Maybe I lost that bet. But I sure made a pile of reward money. Those men I told Sheriff Jones about had a price on their heads. And since I helped Sheriff Jones find them, he gave me the reward."

"That's great, Joe," Lem said. "And you didn't see any ghosts?"

"Only if those two convicts turn out to be dead," Joe said. He took a long, slow puff on his cigar. A frown passed suddenly over Joe's face. He remembered the strange girl with the lantern that had helped him in the woods.

Just then, the door opened and someone came in. Joe looked up, and the cigar almost fell from his mouth.

"Hello, miss," he finally managed to say. "I didn't get a chance to thank you for your help last night."

The young girl gave Joe a blank stare

and shook her head. "I don't know what you're talking about, mister. I've never seen you before."

"But I don't get it," Joe said, feeling strange all of a sudden. "Don't you remember helping me last night in the woods? You were holding a lantern and you—"

"Hey, take it easy, Joe," Mason said. "Let me introduce you to one of my cousins, Sarah Mae. You couldn't have seen her before, Joe. She just arrived this morning from up north."

Joe shook his head as he kept staring at Sarah Mae. He didn't know what to think.

"But maybe you thought you saw her," Mason went on. "Haven't you ever seen that picture of my aunt, Lou Ann?" Mason took down a tiny, yellow photograph that had been stuck to the wall

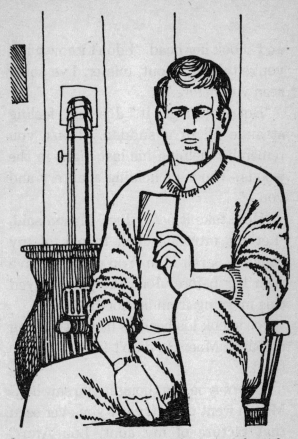

"No!" Joe screamed, seeing the face of the girl that had held the lantern.

behind the cash register.

"Sarah Mae looks just like her," Mason said.

Joe's hands trembled as he took the picture. "No!" he screamed, seeing the face of the girl that had held the lantern. "It can't be!"

Sam and Lem looked at each other and nodded their heads. They knew that Joe Gibbs was well on his way to becoming a believer.

The Animal's Revenge

What I'm about to tell you is quite strange. I would not believe it myself if someone told me.

It happened a few years ago. I was a young boy then. I thought I was tough. I went hunting a lot with my .22.

Usually, I stalked squirrels and rabbits. But this time I wanted to hunt big game. I was going to shoot my first deer.

I told no one where I was going. I borrowed my dad's big old Winchester rifle. That gun was too big for me. I couldn't even hold it steady to my shoulder. I'd have to prop the barrel on a tree branch to shoot straight.

I struck off from the road onto a path. It wasn't much of a path. The pine trees were very thick. Not much light got through, so the forest floor was almost bare. It made cross-country travel easy.

I walked on and came across a stream. It was cold and clear as it bubbled over the rocks. I splashed some water on my face and took a drink. I sat there next to the stream. Its gurgling and gushing made me feel good. I was starting to doze when I heard a noise.

Slowly, I opened my eyes. There, on the bank, was a stag. Its antlers were huge. I couldn't believe my luck. The very thing I was looking for had come right to me.

It drank for a while, then looked up. It looked right at me. We stared at each other for a long time. It didn't seem afraid at all.

Very slowly, I lifted the rifle to my shoulder. I propped the barrel on one knee. Still, the stag watched. I was moving so slowly it all seemed unreal.

I took careful aim. There was no hurry. *Easy*, I said to myself. *Easy now. Squeeze the trigger slowly. Slowly. That's it. Just a gentle pressure . . . Ouch!*

BOOM! The big gun went off. The bullet hit the opposite bank. The stag bounded away. I had missed! It took me a few seconds to figure it out. Something had hit my head.

Clunk! A large pine cone just missed my head. I looked up. Some squirrels were dashing about high in the trees above me. I saw another cone on its way down. I ducked out of the way. *Clunk!* It hit the rock where I had been sitting.

Were those squirrels trying to hit me? It seemed impossible. Squirrels didn't think like that. But it was a very strange accident.

I didn't spend much time thinking about the pine cones. I had to go after that stag.

I followed the hoof prints on the forest floor. In one spot, the stag had stopped to eat. The ground had been pawed. At times, I could hear the animal ahead of me. Everything would be still, then I'd hear it crashing away.

A large pine cone just missed my head.

The stag was headed for the high country. I was short of breath and sweating. The stag was taking me on quite a climb. I stopped for a second to rest.

There was crashing to the left behind me. I froze, listening—nothing. I turned completely around, peering through the trees—nothing. I started on the trail again, when suddenly, the stag took off in front of me. I could see its white tail. I got so excited, I took a few quick shots at it. Of course, they were all wide.

Crash! Something ran through the brush behind me. I gave a start. I thought, *What's going on? Are you back there, Mr. Stag? Are you back behind me again?*

I didn't like what I found. There were hoof prints all right. But there were paw prints, too—a mountain lion's. My first thought was, *Well that explains it. This old stag is running from the two of us. That's why it's all over the place.* But then I began to wonder. Just who was the lion after – Mr. Stag or me?

I'd like to say I kept cool. I didn't. I was scared, and I felt very much alone. That heavy Winchester wasn't much comfort anymore. Well, I panicked. I'd hear a noise and I'd shoot at it. Then I'd run like crazy away from it.

I don't know how long I ran. It seemed like forever. I had a pain in my side. It hurt to breathe.

Suddenly, I stumbled out of the forest into a clearing. It was about the size of a football field. Wildflowers made it all yellow and purple. On three sides of the space was forest. At the far end stood a high bluff.

I collapsed in the clearing. The air was

cool, crisp, and thin. I couldn't seem to get my breath.

I closed my eyes. The earth under me was soft, warm. Did I sleep? I don't think so, but I'm not sure. When I sat up I thought I was dreaming. Surely it was a dream! I was surrounded. Animals stood on all four sides of the clearing. There were all kinds of animals, big and small. There were elk and moose and deer. There were bears and mountain lions. There were raccoons and foxes and wolves. There were squirrels and chipmunks and rabbits. The trees, I could see, were filled with birds.

Slowly, two figures came forward. A mountain lion approached on one side. A large stag loomed on the other. They came closer and closer. About three feet before me, they stopped. The lion growled while the stag snorted and pawed the

A mountain lion approached on one side.

earth. Suddenly, all the animals were making noise, chirping and hooting and bellowing and snorting! The noise was deafening! I kept looking from the lion to the stag. Which would go for me first?

Silence! At once, everything was quiet. I was watching the stag. It put its head up and looked toward the bluff. So did the lion.

I followed their gaze. There on the bluff stood a man. He had gray hair and a beard. He was dressed like a woodsman, in flannel and denim. He had a large staff in his left hand. Three times, the staff hit the rock where he stood. Each blow echoed over the space. Then the man spoke in a booming voice. I couldn't understand the words. Some of it sounded like a language. Some of it was just squeals and whistles. The man made sweeping gestures with his right hand. Every so often, he'd bring the staff down on the rock. BOOM!

The animals listened. Whatever they heard impressed them. The lion began to slink off toward the forest. The stag trotted away. Before it left, it looked at me. It stared right into me. I felt afraid and ashamed.

Then all the animals turned into the forest and vanished. I was left alone with the man on the bluff. He pointed his staff at me. "You!" he thundered. "You are not wanted here."

"Yes, sir," I replied. I could hardly speak.

"What?" he asked. "Louder! Speak up!"

"Yes, sir!" I shouted. "Thank you, sir! You saved my life, sir. Thank you!" I was truly grateful. The man just stared at me for a long time. He seemed to be

"You!" the man thundered.
"You are not wanted here."

making up his mind.

Finally he said, "Go away! Leave this place. . . . If you ever return, come un-armed. Hunters are not welcome here."

"Yes, sir," I shouted. I turned to go. "May I leave now, sir?" I thought I'd better ask. I wasn't taking any chances.

"Go!" he bellowed. "Go and beware! I cannot protect all such fools as you."

With that, he vanished. I rubbed my eyes and pinched myself, but I was awake. I didn't tell Dad when I got home. I didn't tell anybody till now. I've been back to the forest. But I go without a gun now. And sometimes, if I listen hard, I hear the BOOM of a wooden staff striking stone.